GRACE NOBLE

MURDER BY GRACE

SHANNON SPRUILL

SMS WRITE ON PUBLISHING, LLC

Shannon Spruill/SMS Write On Publishing, LLC

3843 Union Road

Suite 15 #141

Cheektowaga, NY 14225

www.smswriteonpub.com

Grace Noble/Shannon Spruill. -- 1st ed.

ISBN 978-1-7320234-0-6

First and foremost, I give thanks to God!
Dedicated to my cheerleaders; Magic, Derek & Patrick
Thank you to my Literary Agent – Latonya "The Diva"
Granberry

Ninja - a person who excels in a particular skill or activity.

CONTENTS

GRACE

I was staring out the window looking at the moon illuminate the street while drinking a glass of 2007 Sassicaia (Cabernet Sauvignon). It was a quiet and peaceful night. I sat thinking about the new case I got today. A woman killed her abusive boyfriend. They should have been applauding her, but instead, we had to arrest her. She claimed it was self-defense, but she shot him in the back. After we completed our investigation, she would be going to jail.

I had everything a woman at the age of forty-two could want. A beautiful four-bedroom home in Hempstead, Long Island. I am a detective with the NYPD Crime Scene Unit. Our unit is part of the NYPD Detective Bureau's Forensic investigation division. We are responsible for all forensic investigations of murders and sexual assaults. We cover all of New York City's five boroughs. I have no children and no husband. I never wanted either. I am an only child and a daddy's girl. My father is a Judge, and my mother is a school administrator. My hobby is watching any crime drama on television that I can find. I enjoy trying to solve murders, and I am usually on point. My all-time favorite movie is Dial M for Murder.

I was brought out of my trance by my doorbell. Who is ringing my doorbell at 10 pm? I was not up for any company. I walked over and looked out the peephole. I recognized that eye staring back at me through the peephole. It was Maxwell, my neighbor from two houses down the street. Maxwell moved into the neighborhood about two years ago, and it seemed like I was the first neighbor to catch his attention. He was very nerdy and stayed to himself. Nice guy but he was looking for more than I was willing to give him. I opened the door slightly and faked a tired look on my face.

"Hey Maxwell, I was just going to bed, I have an early morning. What's up?"

He hesitated for a moment as if he forgot his words. "I just wanted to make sure you were ok, I heard the police siren and just wanted to check on you".

The police were not in front of my house so why did he find it necessary to check on me?

"Well I am fine, and I will talk to you tomorrow." I closed the door gently because I did not want to give him the impression that I was slamming the door in his face.

I did not want to be bothered, but I did not want to be rude about it. Maxwell Harrington was a little strange, and I could not put my finger on it, but my radar said bad news. I grabbed my case file and my glass of wine and went to my bedroom.

My cell phone woke me up. I looked at the time, and it was 5:30 am.

"Hello"

"Wake up sleeping beauty!! We have work to do. We have a 187 in Brooklyn. Meet me at 75 Ocean Avenue, right across the street from Prospect Park."

"Damn, I was hoping for a slow day. I will be there as soon as possible."

"See you there, Sunshine!"

Nick Moretti was my partner, and we have been partners for six years. Nick is an excellent forensic detective, and we work well together. Nick is Italian and has a thick Italian accent. He would take a bullet for me, and I would do the same for him. I needed to jump into the shower, and I would just have to light up the cherries into Brooklyn.

When I arrived at the scene, I was not expecting what I saw. The crime scene was secured. It was in a first-floor apartment. There are various patterns that we use to assure complete coverage of the crime scene. We decided to do a zone search. Nick was the CSI in charge, and he divided the crime scene into sectors, and each team member took one area. There were two dead bodies, and there was blood everywhere. This murder scene indicated a ruthless attack. We checked to see if windows and doors were locked and any sign of forced entry. There was none, which suggested to us that they knew the assailant or assailants and let them in. They were not aware of what would happen next.

"Well, Grace looks like we will be here for a while. What is your initial take? A drug deal has gone bad?"

"No, because they did not take the money. If it were a bad drug deal, they would have taken the money. Think about it Nick; There was no forced entry. Victims are a male and female. Bodies found in the bedroom and both were naked. The other interesting fact is the male victim took the most abuse. He was shot and then repeatedly stabbed. The assailant was someone who was extremely angry. The woman only had one puncture wound. The woman has a stab wound in the

4

neck. It was as if the woman was being punished even though he loved her. You get where I am going, Nick? This murder was a love triangle, and these two got caught in the act."

"Wow, you make some valid points. Once we get identifications on the victims, we can check and see who the significant other may be."

"And that is your killer!"

"I guess you do have a point. The only reason that I suggested a bad drug deal is because this building is notorious for drug activity. But leave it to you to crack the case. After we finish up here, let's grab a bite to eat."

"That sounds good to me." It took us a couple of hours to bag up all the evidence.

Since we were in Brooklyn, Nick and I decided to go to Juniors for lunch.

"Grace, are there times that you wish you were doing something else? Maybe a lawyer or even a Judge, like your pops?"

"No, because I am happy doing just what I am doing. I know many people would think that I get tired of seeing the dead bodies, but I enjoy the investigative side. I love figuring out what happened. Every crime scene presents a new challenge for me, and I love it. What about you Nick?"

"Well, I don't have the same zeal for the job as you

do. Don't get me wrong, I like my job but seeing the dead bodies does wear on me."

Nick was a great partner, but there were times he overlooked the smallest of clues when investigating a crime scene. I often ask myself, do any of these criminals give any thought to the crimes they commit? So many crimes that I investigate, I can figure out a way to get away with the crime. I guess that is because I am an investigator. Is there such a thing as the perfect crime? Some criminals don't get caught, but their crimes do not go undetected. Can you commit a crime that is so perfect that it does not seem like a crime was committed? I often thought like a criminal to figure out some of my crime scenes.

"Hey Grace, you seem to be lost in your world."

"Sorry about that, I just had a few things on my mind. I have a question for you; have you ever thought about jumping to the other side? Like becoming a vigilante?"

"Wow, what a strange question."

"Just wondering and please don't make me your number one suspect the next time there is a vigilante murder!"

Nick chuckled because he would never suspect me of committing any crime. Our trust of one another was solid.

"Well, I have never thought about jumping to the other side even though there are some criminals I would like to put a hurting on."

Before we could finish our conversation, my cell phone rang. It was another case, but it was in Queens this time. We stayed busy covering the five boroughs.

2

NOT MY MOM

I got home around 8 pm and I was exhausted. I was sorting through my mail when my phone rang.

"Hello"

"Hey baby girl"

The only time my dad called me Grace was if he was upset with me. He always calls me baby girl. But there was something about his voice tonight that indicated that something was wrong.

"Hey, dad, what's the matter?" "

I am at the hospital with your mother. I need you to stay calm. Your mother was attacked and robbed this evening on her way home from a school board meeting."

"What hospital are you at?"

"We are at St. Francis Hospital."

My parents live in Old Westbury, New York and St. Francis was about 13 minutes from their home and 24 minutes from mine.

"I am on my way, and I will get the details when I get there. How is she doing?"

Baby girl, it is bad. She got stabbed multiple times. They are prepping her for surgery. Get here as soon as you can. Love you."

I was in shock and moving as if I was in a trance. I called Nick, and he said he would meet me at the hospital. Nick was very close to my parents, and they loved Nick and treated him as part of the family. My father was African American and born in North Carolina. My mother was Italian, and they met when he moved to New York. I heard many stories about the racism they faced as an interracial couple. They endured and stayed the course. Theirs was true love.

My father is a big man who stands six feet 5 inches and weighs 280 pounds. However, as I walked down the hospital corridor and spotted him, he looked so small and diminished. Without saying a word, we embraced. I did not want to let him go. Nick was already there, and I hugged him also.

"Thank you for being here Nick."

"Don't mention it."

I wanted to get details from my dad, but I thought I

needed to be his daughter at this moment and not a detective. I would let him give me the details when he was ready. We just sat in silence. About 2 hours passed and the doctor came to speak to us.

"Mr. Noble, we have good news; we stopped the bleeding. We will keep your wife in ICU to monitor her, but I do expect a full recovery."

"Can I see her?"

"Your wife is heavily sedated, so you can't see her right now. We will let you know when you can see her."

My father shook hands with the doctor.

"Baby girl I don't have any details as to what happened. When I got to your mom, she was unconscious. The police told me that someone called and reported a woman lying next to a car unconscious and bleeding. When the police got to the scene, your mother's purse was on the ground, and her credit cards and money were missing. Why couldn't they just take the money and leave her alone?"

"Listen, dad; we just need to focus on taking care of mom. I will talk with the lead detectives and see what evidence they were able to collect."

I could not convince my father to go home and get some rest. Nick walked with me as I was leaving.

"Partner, you know you are too close to this. Let me see what I can find out."

I was too emotionally drained to put up a fight with Nick.

"See what you can find out and I am going home."

Over the next few days, my mother showed remarkable improvements. She did not remember much of what happened and I did not want to press her for information. I was just glad that she was improving. I would try to get to the hospital daily, just to give my dad a break.

"Grace, you don't have to come up here so often. I know you have work to do and I will be ok. I wish I could tell you more about what happened but it all happened so fast. You know I would have given them the purse if that was all they wanted. Honestly, it was like the one guy was intent on killing me. I don't feel like it was really about the money."

"What makes you say that mom?" She closed her eyes as if she was imaging it happening all over again.

"It was just his body language. The contents of my purse were just an afterthought to him. I could have been delirious with fear but that is a gut feeling that I had."

"Mom, I can't imagine anyone wanting to intentionally harm you. You are probably over thinking everything. Enough talk about that, we are going to concentrate on you getting better. You know I love you?"

"I know you do and I love you more."

I always felt that my mother was the nicest person in the world. If we were together and she saw a homeless person, she would buy them something to eat and then start a conversation with them. This came natural to her and she was always concerned with other's wellbeing. When I was a little girl, she often told me to be compassionate and never be judgmental.

"Grace, I don't want you to obsess with finding the guys responsible for the attack. I know how you are. Just thank God that I am ok and find it in your heart to forgive them."

Only my mother could be talking about forgiving the guy that stabbed her.

"I am staying away from the investigation and forgiveness comes easier for you mom. I still find it hard to forgive something like this."

"Well I am going to pray for you like I always do. You might have better success if you start going to church."

We looked at each other and just started laughing. I was raised in the church but seeing death and destruction every day on my job, serving God was hard for me. I would not say I did not believe in God, I just did not understand him, and I guess my faith was not strong enough to trust Him. As I sat there with my mother, my phone rang.

"Hello"

"Hey Sunshine! I have some info for you. Can we meet?"

"Sure, do you want to meet me at my house?"

"Yeah, that will work. I will see you in an hour."

When I got home, Nick was already there waiting in his car. He got out and we both went inside.

"Do you want a glass of wine?"

"I would prefer a beer."

I got him a beer and we sat down.

"What do you have for me?"

"I actually have a suspect. We were able to lift finger-prints from the crime scene and we got a hit. Jose Lopez, a gangbanger and he has a long rap sheet. No ID on the second suspect. We are bringing him in for questioning."

I was glad to hear that they identified one of the suspects, but I knew he would not suffer for the pain that he has caused my mother. I loved my job, but I had a problem with our legal system. Our legal system is not tough enough on criminals. But that's a battle for another day.

"Thanks for your help with this Nick. Not sure what I would do without you."

He smiled and gave me a kiss on the forehead.

"Listen sunshine, I have to run. I actually have a date. Can you imagine a woman going out with me?"

We both bust out laughing. I walked Nick to the door.

"See you tomorrow."

It was hard to understand why Nick could not find the right woman. He was handsome but for some reason, he had terrible luck with women. The closest he came to marriage was with a girl named Joyce and that was a bitter breakup. I never pried into his love life.

3

PAMELA

$\mathcal{I}$ sat on my living couch with a glass of wine thinking about Jose Lopez. Who would miss him? Did he have a family? Would the world be a better place without him? I had to get over these feelings and let the legal system handle Jose Lopez. I was just grateful that my mother was making a full recovery. Before I could finish my wine, the phone rings.

"Hello"

"Hey Grace, we got a hot one. Queens - 2548 100th Street - Triple homicide and we have a victim or suspect at the scene. Meet you there."

"Ok, I am on my way."

Good thing I did not get undressed. When I got to the scene, I was taken aback because I was not expecting to find a three year amongst the victims. In all the years of doing my job, it was always difficult to see a dead child. It looked like a possible drive-by because all victims were outside of an apartment building. It looks like it is possible the infant was an innocent bystander.

"Hey Nick, what do we have so far?"

"Still collecting evidence and there is a young lady in the back of that patrol car over there. Not sure if she is a victim or a suspect. She won't talk, but maybe you can give it a try."

I walked over to the patrol car and showed my badge. I got into the back seat.

"Hi, my name is Detective Noble. We are trying to figure out what happened here, and it looks like you might be the only one who can shed some light on this situation. I am sure you are scared, but we need your help."

"I am not scared. I just would not talk to anyone but you."

That was a bizarre response because I did not know this girl and I was pretty sure that she did not know me.

"I don't think I know you."

"You don't know me, but I know you, Grace."

I did not recognize this girl and how the hell did she know my name?

"How do you know my name?"

She went silent on me again.

"What is your name?" "

I did not do this, and I did not see who did it. When I got here, they were already dead. And my name is Pamela."

This line of questioning was going nowhere, and I still wanted to know how she knew my name.

"Pamela, can you tell me how you knew my name?"

She went silent on me again. I got out of the car and walked over to where Nick was standing.

"I did not get anything out of her. She states that she discovered the bodies and they were already dead. But there was something strange; she knew my name."

"Do you know the girl?"

"No, I don't know her, and when I asked her how she knew my name, she went silent on me. It was weird, and it was little unsettling."

"Don't make too much out of it. She probably heard one of the officers or even me calling your name."

Nick was probably right, but for some reason, it was bothering me that she knew my name.

"Oh, by the way, the double homicide in Brooklyn turned out to be a jealous husband. When we brought the husband in for questioning, he broke down and confessed. You were right on point."

"Yeah, I knew it. Pay attention, and you could learn some things"

We enjoyed a good laugh. We learned a long time ago that we had to laugh a lot to avoid losing our sanity. We finished up our investigation, and I went home.

I poured a glass of wine and ran a hot bath. I just wanted to relax but I kept thinking about the fact that the girl knew my name. How was that possible? She had to hear my name from one of the other officers. That had to be it. I started thinking about Jose Lopez and how I could make him pay. How could I eliminate him and go unnoticed? I know I could pull it off if I took my time to plan it out. I could actually commit murder and I was confident that I could masterfully pull it off. I had to be crazy to even be thinking about committing murder. I came close to committing murder about three years ago. I was investigating the murder of three-year-old little girl. The suspect was her stepfather. The mother and stepfather got into an argument. Both were heroin addicts. The stepfather injected the little girl with a fatal dose of heroin. When I was arresting that scumbag, I asked him why? He responded that he had to let his wife know he meant business and he did not think it would kill the little girl. At that moment, I wanted to pull out my revolver and blow out his brains. I did not often get rattled on the job but when it came to children, that was my weakness. After I took my bath, I decided I would go to bed and get some much-needed sleep. Just as I was dozing off to sleep my phone rang.

"Hello."

There was a slight hesitation from the other end of the phone.

"Hi, is this Grace?"

"Yes, this is Grace. Who am I speaking to?"

"This is Pamela." There was a very awkward silence.

"Is this Pamela from earlier this evening at the murder scene in Queens?"

"Yes, that would be me." I became instantly upset.

"How the hell did you get my phone number?" I took a breath to allow her to answer.

"It was not hard but that is not important right now." I quickly interrupted her.

"What the hell do you mean that it is not important? Yes, it is important, and this conversation is ending now." Before I could hang up, she said something that caught my attention;

"Jose Lopez should pay for his sins! No one is above the law." Now instead of anger, I was feeling uneasy.

"Ok Pamela, you really need to tell me what is going on. How do you know about Jose Lopez?" There was a long pause and then she spoke.

"In due time, you will see but for now just give

thought to the fact that Jose Lopez should be put to death." She hung up the phone before I could say a word.

What was going on and how the hell did she know my name and number. Most importantly, how did she know about Jose Lopez? I quickly dialed Nick's number. Phone rang five times and I was about to hang up when he answered.

"Hey, do you know what time it is?" I didn't bother to check the time, but I looked over at my clock and it was 2 am.

"I am so sorry to call so late but something very strange just happened. That girl from the Queens' crime scene called me tonight."

"That is not too crazy because these days you just need a name and it is easy to get a phone number. She could have called the station and said she needed to speak to you. She called your cell phone, right?"

"Yes, she did."

"Ok that is your work number so not so odd. What did she want?"

"She did not say. She just said that Jose Lopez should pay for his sins. Now do you agree, that is odd?"

"Ok, that might qualify as odd. There is not much we can figure out tonight, so how about I meet you down at the station tomorrow and we can further investigate."

"I guess you have a point. I will meet you at the station around 8:30."

"And listen Grace; get some sleep because you know there is a logical explanation for all of this and we will figure it out." I heard what Nick was saying but something inside of me felt differently.

I woke at 5 a.m. and took a shower. After I took my shower, I went to the kitchen to make some coffee, and as I was passing through the living room, I noticed a piece of paper that was slipped under the door. It was a note from Maxwell letting me know that he stopped by and if I needed anything, let him know. I would have to eventually have a talk with Maxwell and tell him that I do not need a guardian angel. He was starting to get a little out of control. I was not his girlfriend, and it was time to put an end to his crush. I finished my coffee and decided to go to the station early and wait for Nick. I was completing some paperwork and decided to see if I could find anything out about Pamela. It was bothering me that she knew things about me and I did not know her. I could not find any information on her. I was interrupted by my ringing phone.

"Hello."

"Hey sunshine, we got a body. It is the girl from the other night, Pamela."

"What happened?"

"Bullet right between the eyes." It took me a minute to process what I just heard.

Now I will never get answers to my questions. Something about all of this was just not sitting right with me. Pamela's body found in an alleyway in Flatbush Brooklyn. There was not a lot of evidence. Whoever shot her was a professional and knew what they were doing. But what was this girl involved in and why was she murdered. I knew there was so much more to this girl and I will never have the opportunity to find out.

"Nick, you know this was not just a random murder and the fact that she knew me, and she knew about Jose Lopez means that this is not over."

"Listen, Grace, try not to obsess with this because I am sure there is a logical explanation. We have not been able to locate Lopez, but we have an APB out for him, and I will let you know once we have him in custody."

"OK. I am going home, so you know where to find me." I just needed some downtime because I could not shake this feeling I had.

When I got home, Maxwell was waiting at my door. I was now getting very annoyed with Maxwell. Enough is enough, and this had to stop.

"Hey, Maxwell. Why are you here?"

"I was just stopping by to check on you."

"Listen, I am not trying to be mean, but you have to

stop coming over uninvited. I do not need or want your protection. I am a detective, and I can handle myself just fine. Please stop showing up on my doorstep. I am not trying to hurt your feelings, but this is not cool." He looked at me without any emotion.

"No problem; I will not stop by anymore." As he turned to walk away he mumble under his breath, "Pamela felt the same way."

"Hey, what did you say? How do you know about Pamela?"

He did not turn around as he answered me.

"I did not say anything, and I don't know what you are talking about." I know what I heard or what I thought I heard. I decided not to pursue him and just let him leave. I was allowing this Pamela situation consume me.

4

HARD TO SAY GOODBYE

Over the next couple of days, Nick and I stayed busy, and I thought less about Pamela. Maxwell kept his word, and I did not see him lurking around. There was a part of me that felt bad for being so stern with him, but it was necessary. I was up early getting ready to head to the station, and my phone rang.

"Hello"

"Baby girl I am at the hospital with your mother. She woke up this morning bleeding from one of the stab wounds in her chest. I tried to apply direct pressure for five minutes, but it did not stop the bleeding. She was complaining of chills and was shaking uncontrollably. She had a fever of 103 degrees. I brought her to the emergency room for an examination. The doctor thinks it is an infection, but I don't know any more than that. If you are going to work, I will keep you updated."

"I am on my way to the hospital. There is no way I could go to work. Besides, I would get nothing done worrying about mom. Are you at St. Francis?"

"Yes, I am, and we are still in the emergency room."

"Ok, I will see you in a few minutes."

When I arrived at the hospital, I saw my father sitting at the end of the hall with his hand covering his face as if he was crying. A doctor was standing in front of him. I quickened my pace to get to my father.

"Hey, Dad, what's going on?" When he lifted his head, I could see that he had been crying.

"Grace, your mother is gone." I could not believe what he just said to me.

There had to be some mistake. She was doing so well after the attack. I turned and looked at the doctor.

"How is this possible?"

The tears were streaming down my face, and I felt like I could not catch my breath. He took me by the arm and led me to the seat next to my father.

"Please have a seat. Because of the large amounts of blood loss your mother sustained, she developed clotting problems, and there was organ failure due to the shock of the blood loss. She also went into cardiac arrest, and we were not able to revive her. I am sorry."

I was numb and in shock. I did not know how to console my father. We just sat side by side in silence. I sent a text to Nick because I could not bring myself to call and utter the words that she is gone. Nick was there as soon as possible. He sat down next to me and just grabbed me and held me while I cried.

"This is now a murder case!"

"Not now sunshine, we will take care of this. I just want you to focus on taking care of your dad. If you need help with any of the arrangements, please let me know. I will be more than happy to assist in any way that I can. I loved her like she was my mom."

"Thank you, Nick, and I will be in touch."

I decided to go home with my dad and spend the rest of the day with him. I handled all the arrangements for my father. I wanted to make sure her home-going celebration was special. Over the next several days, everything was a blur. I was on autopilot. When I woke on the day of the funeral, I was angry. I got up and looked in the mirror. With my right arm, I swept everything off of my dresser and began wrecking my bedroom. I wanted Jose Lopez dead. I did not want him in prison; I wanted him dead. I was in a rage when my doorbell rang. I did not want to answer it, but I knew it was probably Nick. I left my bedroom and closed the door. I did not want Nick to see the aftermath of my rage. I opened the door and let Nick in.

"Hey, how are you holding up?"

"I am good as can be expected. I am going to take a shower and get dressed. Help yourself to coffee." I left Nick and went to get ready for my mother's funeral.

There was standing room only at the church. I was so thankful for the show of support from my brothers and sisters in blue. NYPD showed up in full force, along with Judges and politicians. I just wanted this nightmare to end. The service was beautiful, and everyone gathered at my father's house afterwards. My father was holding up the best he could, but it looked like he aged by ten years overnight. I know he would be empty without my mother, but I already made up in my mind that I would make sure I was there for him to help him through. As the guest started leaving, it was Dad, Nick and I left. We spent time reminiscing about mom and the happier times.

"Hey, you two, I am exhausted physically and emotionally. I am going to bed. Baby girl make sure all the locks are on when you leave. Love you both and I will talk to you tomorrow."

"Love you too dad." That just left Nick and me.

"Nick, I am angry. I am angry!"

As I was saying this, I was clinching the cushion on the couch. Nick moved closer and embraced me.

"Listen, sweetheart; I know that you are in a lot of pain right now and I am so sorry that you are going through this and you are allowed to be angry."

Nick had no idea what was running through my head. Jose Lopez had to die. He had to pay for what he did to my mother.

"I will be ok. I think I will go home. I just need some time alone."

When I got home, there was a note under my door. I knew it was from Maxwell.

Hey Grace, I know you said not to bother you, but I just wanted to tell you that I am sorry about your mother and if you need anything, please let me know. Maxwell

I could not get upset with him because this time I believed he meant well. I started thinking about a leave of absence. Nick was very supportive, but I knew he would not be happy working with anyone else. I was mentally exhausted, but there was work to be done. I logged into our police database and began a search on Jose Lopez. I checked for outstanding arrest warrants and his criminal history with the NCIC database. NCIC is the National

Crime Information Center, and it is a computerized index of criminal justice information (i.e., criminal record history information, fugitives, stolen properties, missing persons). Of course, Jose Lopez was in the database. There was a temporary felony want to be issued in connection with my mother's assault or should I say her murder. I was sure that would change to a permanent want. There were three different addresses listed for his residence. I also did a cross check in the NYPD Gang database. I started an encrypted file on my computer to save the information that I collected. I decided I was going to submit a request for a three-month leave of absence. I would not get any resistance especially after the death of my mother. They would probably recommend time off to get me together mentally. Three months was plenty of time to locate and survey Jose's daily activities and put a plan in place. There was that tiny voice inside of me saying, what are you doing?

5

BETRAYAL

I was able to locate Jose's daily hang out spot and where he was staying. He was living with a girl, whom I assume was his latest girlfriend. There were 4 kids in the home also. He was a low-level drug dealer and was a member of the La Raza Nation. La Raza is a street gang that started in Chicago in 1973. Green, white and red are their colors. I began surveillance of Jose and got familiar with his comings and goings. My plan was straightforward; Kidnap, torture and death. I could not recognize the person I was becoming but this needed to be done. I pinpointed the time of day that he would most likely be alone. I just needed to decide how I would go about abducting him. I used an alias to rent a small warehouse in Queens. I took care of the transaction by phone and online. When the rental agent asked to meet with me, I said I did not have any availability, but I was willing to pay 90 days in advance. Meeting me was not an issue after that. Next, I had to get a vial of succinylcholine. This was going to be the final stage and the drug used to suck the air out of Jose Lopez. Succinylcholine is perfect because it is a neuromuscular paralytic drug and it paralyses all the muscle in the body including those used for breathing and eventually asphyxiation. I chose this drug because it is the perfect murder weapon and it metabolizes almost immediately into the by-products succinic acid and choline. Both of these products are normal to the body and will go unnoticed during an autopsy. I was covering all the bases and making sure that nothing could be traced back to me. I decided to call my dad because I was trying to make sure that I talked with him daily. He was doing well but I could hear the loneliness in his voice. He was not the same, which was to be expected after losing your soul mate.

"Hi Dad, how are you doing?"

"I am fine baby girl and you don't have to call me every day. I know you have your life and I am adjusting to my new life."

I loved my dad for putting up a brave front, but I knew he was not doing well. He was heartbroken.

"Listen dad, you are part of the life that I have, and you will not be able to stop me from calling you every day. It sets me at ease to hear your voice. I know you miss her because I have a large hole in my heart and it is important for us to lean on one another. I love you dearly." There was a brief silence. It was as if he was deciding if it was ok to open up and talk about his feelings.

"Grace, I am lost without your mother. I keep asking myself, how am I going to go on without her. You are the only reason that I am pushing on, but it is so hard. I am hoping with each passing day, it will get easier. I am also angry at the young man responsible for your mother's attack. I don't want the anger to consume me but between the loneliness and anger, I feel like I am going crazy." I just let him talk because this is what he needed. "I am tired of crying because it is not productive, and nothing changes. Your mom is not coming back to me and I have to try and come to terms with this new reality." I really did not know what to say.

"Dad, I love you and we will get through this together. Do you want to go to dinner tomorrow night?"

"Yes, but I need to know how you are doing, honestly. I don't want you to do anything crazy. Let the legal system do their job." My father knew me very well, but he probably would not recognize this woman planning to murder the man who murdered her mother.

"I took a leave of absence and I am leaving this investigation to someone else. I am doing good, but I still have my bad days. And I too am angry, but I believe it is a natural emotion under the circumstances. I love you and you think about where you want to go for dinner tomorrow."

"Love you too and I will talk to you later."

I hung up and sat there thinking maybe I needed to let this plan of revenge go and try to work on the healing process. I quickly dismissed that notion. Jose Lopez had to pay with his life.

The following morning, I was parked across the street from one of Jose's hangouts. He was standing in front of a corner store talking to two other guys. Every so often a car would pull up and he we go over and have a brief conversation. He would then go in the back of the building and come back to the car and hand them something. I know these were drug deals, but I was not here to bust him for drug sales. He did this until late into the afternoon. He left around 3 pm and went home. I sat outside of his house for about one hour before he exited. He walked back to the store by himself. Over the next week he stuck to this basic routine. He always walked by himself in the afternoon when leaving home and heading back to the spot he conducted business. I planned on surveying him for another week just to confirm the established pattern. This was going to be my opportunity and I needed to make sure everything was perfect.

I went to the warehouse to make sure everything was in place. There was still a small voice telling me to stop this madness, but I was determined to ignore that voice. I had been watching Jose for two weeks and I would put my plan in action within the next couple of days. I decided to go home when something very strange caught my eye. A car pulled up and Jose got in. That was not the weird thing. The vehicle was Nick's car. What the hell was Nick doing talking to Jose and why was he not arresting him? My first instinct was to rush over there and demand some answers. But I didn't because something was not right, and I did not want to give him a chance to make up a lie to cover his tracks. Could Nick be on drugs? Hell no! I knew Nick well, or at least I thought I did. What other reason would he have for socializing with this murderer? They sat in the car for approximately 20 minutes before Nick left.

I went straight home, and when I got there, I felt like I could not breathe. Once I got inside of my house, I started hyperventilating. I sat down and tried to get my breathing under control. I was not sure what was going on, but I felt so betrayed. Nick stopped by later in the day, but I did not let on that I saw him with Jose.

"Hey sunshine, you seem a little distant tonight. Are you ok?" I needed to pull it together because I did not need Nick to think that anything was wrong.

"I am fine Nick, I just was thinking about dad. He is putting up such a front and I know that he is hurting and lost without my mother. I am just worrying about him." I think I did a good job of recovering and keeping Nick from knowing something was up.

Listen, your dad will be fine. He is going through the normal grieving process and I am sure he misses your mom. I have some work to finish up at the station, so I am going to go now." I was so glad he was leaving.

I could not look at him the same anymore and I did not trust him. I was determined to find out what was going on and why did it involve my mother.

"I will call you later. And thanks for everything." I walked him to the door and he kissed me on the check.

When he left, I closed and locked my door. I suppose while I am torturing Jose, I can find out what is his involvement with Nick. I spent the rest of the evening going over the final details. Wednesday, I did a last surveillance to make sure nothing had changed much. I decide this would happen the following day. As I sat there watching the house, Jose came out and a little girl ran to the door and hugged and kissed him. I wondered was this his child and thought about the fact that I would be taking this child's father from her. I tried to shake this feeling because he stole a mother from her child and a wife from her husband. In my mind, I was saving this little girl from the monster called dad. I drove off and went home.

6

REVENGE TASTE SO SWEET

I woke up Thursday morning feeling anxious. Today was the day I have waited for it since the day my mother died. I took a shower and made a cup of coffee. I sat there going over my plan in my head to make sure I did not leave anything out. I left out at 10 am and did my usual surveillance. I would intercept Jose later in the day when he leaves his house. I watched his every move and at around 3:30 pm he had not left his home yet. I was beginning to worry that his routine changed today. It was 4:30 pm and I was about to go when I saw him leaving his house, and it was now show-time. I pulled off and drove up right next to where he was walking.

"Hey buddy, can you tell me where I can buy some

weed around here?" He gave me a once over and walked over to my car.

"Are you the police? You look like five O."

"Wow, I don't know if that is a compliment or an insult. I am not the police. Just point me in the right direction, and I will leave you alone." He hesitated for just a quick second and then he opened my car door and got in.

"What is pretty lady like you doing out here by herself driving around?" I reached into my pocket and pulled out my revolver.

"Now put your hands up on the dashboard." I reached into his pocket and removed his pistol. I took a pair of handcuffs and tossed them at him. "Now put on those bracelets and don't try anything foolish because I am looking for a reason to blow your head off."

"Hey, be cool. What have I done to you lady? Are you robbing me? I would be careful because you don't know who you are messing with." I took another pair of hand-cuffs and wrapped those around and cuffed him to the door handle.

"I am warning you not to try anything stupid. I will fill you in on all the details shortly. For now, shut your mouth until we get to our destination."

It was a 30-minute ride to the warehouse in Queens.

It was in a very secluded part of town. It was blocks of nothing but warehouses. I walked him into the ware-house at gunpoint. There was a large metal table centered between two concrete poles. I made him lay down on the table and handcuffed his arms to the poles.

"You have not said a word since you drove me to this place. This is not very comfortable laying here in this position. Talk to me please?" I pulled up a chair next to the table and sat down.

"Do you know Pauline Noble?" I paused to let him answer.

"No, never heard the name."

"She was married to Thomas Noble. I am positive you know her." Jose began twisting his arms and hands as if this motion would magically open the handcuffs.

"Listen, lady, I don't know what this is all about, but I don't know this lady or her husband. Enough is enough, and you need to let me go."

"She was my mother, and she recently died. She was murdered." He stopped twisting and squirming, and for a split second, he seemed to be interested in what I had to say.

"I am sorry for your loss but what does that have to do with me?"

"She was robbed and stabbed several times. She died

from complications related to the stab wounds." At that instance, he knew.

"You look as though you have seen a ghost. I guess you know my mother after all. She did not deserve to be stabbed and left in the street for dead. I guess you know why you are here now. You will pay for what you did, and you will suffer before you die."

"Look, lady, I am sorry for what I did but killing me is not going to bring your mom back, and you become just as bad as I am. I will turn myself into the police and confess."

"Your begging doesn't change the fact that my mom is dead, and you are still breathing." I got up and picked up the duct tape and tore off a strip and covered his mouth with it.

"You will never feel or understand the loss that I am feeling, but you will feel the pain of your sin."

I had a couple of vials of Midazolam, and I prepared one for injecting Jose. This drug would knock him out. Jose began making jerky movements and squirming. He had no idea what I was about to pump him with which was evident in his moist and overly bright eyes. Within a few minutes after the injection, he was unconscious. I made sure he was secured to the table. There were two poles at the bottom of the table and I used chains to secure his legs. Jose was not going anywhere. This was where he would take his last breath. I left Jose and went home. I took a long hot shower and got dressed to meet my father for dinner.

Dinner with Dad was robotic. We made small talk, but he was not the same man. He was not the same without my mother. I was preoccupied with Jose at the warehouse. We ate our meal in silence until he asked me a question I was not expecting.

"Grace, have you ever thought about killing the man responsible for your mother's death?" I was momentarily stunned.

"Well, dad I would be lying if I said no but I do not dwell on it. I know it has been hard for you and I don't know the magic words to make you feel better. The best I can do is to tell you how much I love you and I am here for you."

"Baby girl, I would never think less of you if you did. I just want you to know that."

What did he know? Did he know what I was doing? Had I slipped up somewhere?

"Dad, don't talk like that. I am a law enforcement officer, and I would never contemplate murder."

"Ok baby girl, but I love you regardless."

It was as if I was talking to a stranger. I believe if he

came face to face with Jose, he would not hesitate to kill him. We finished our dinner in silence. When I got home, there was a message from Nick. I did not feel like speaking to him, but I needed to carry on as usual.

"Hey Nick, what's up?"

"Just checking on you. I have not heard from you and wanted to make sure you were ok." It took everything in me not to hang up the phone.

"I have been good. Just got back from dinner with dad. I have been using this time alone to reflect on the good times with my mother. Nothing personal just needed the alone time."

"That's fine, just wanted to let you know that I am here if you need anything."

"Thanks, Nick and I will talk to you soon."

It was so hard talking to Nick. Not only was I upset, but I was also hurt because I loved Nick as a brother. I felt so betrayed. I would deal with Nick later. I need to get back to Jose. When I got back to the warehouse, Jose was awake staring at the ceiling. I removed the tape from his mouth.

"Where have you been and just how long are you going to keep me here?"

I did not answer him right away. I sat down and pulled a photo album out of my purse.

"I have some photos I want to show you."

"I don't want to see any of your damn photos. You are sick. What do you want from me? I am sorry about what happened to your mother, but I can't bring her back."

I stood up and held the photo album in front of Jose's face.

"These are pictures of my mother. Take a good look at her."

He went to turn his head but stopped to look at the picture of my mother. He stared at it for a moment and for an instant I thought I saw remorse in his eyes.

"Listen, lady, I am so sorry and to be honest with you, I don't want to die. I know what I did was so wrong. Just let me go or call the police and have me arrested."

"You are not going anywhere and believe me when I am done with you; you will be begging me to kill you."

"Do you plan on giving me something to eat or drink?"

I just smiled at him and got up and left. As I drove home, I thought about what I was doing. What I was doing was wrong, and I knew it, but I did not trust the justice system to make Jose pay for his sins. I need to know and see first-hand that he suffered. I could not keep Jose alive much longer for fear of me letting him go. It was the battle between good and evil waging war within me. I just needed to make him suffer one more night and tomorrow I would rid the world of Jose Lopez.

When I got home, I thought about how I would deal with Nick. I thought about confronting him, but that might draw attention to myself as it pertains to Jose. I was not sure how to handle him, but I needed to do something because it was hard to act normal around him. I just could not understand why Nick would be talking to Jose other than to arrest him. After I finished with Jose, I would figure out how to deal with Nick. I was getting ready to run a bath when my doorbell rang. I walked over and looked out the peephole, and I was not surprised to see Maxwell's eye staring back at me. I opened the door and motioned for him to come in.

"Thanks for stopping by and thank you for the nice note you left for me." He sat on the couch with a very nervous look on his face.

"I was so sorry to hear about your mother, and I just wanted to make sure that you were ok. I don't want to be a bother. I just know how tough it is to lose your mother. It was tough for me when I lost my mother. I was very close to my mother. That was six years ago, and it still seems like yesterday."

"Wow, I am so sorry for your loss. So, you can relate

to how I am feeling. I appreciate your concern, and I am sorry if I come off edgy at times."

"No worries at all. I do like you, but I do not want to be pushy. I am happy just being your friend."

I did not want to lead Maxwell on because I think he was just a caring person. But that little voice in my head still warned me to be careful.

"I appreciate your friendship. Would you like a glass of wine?"

"I would love a glass of wine."

We spent the next two hours talking and getting to know each other better. Even though he was not my type, I did enjoy the company because it was a distraction. We talked for two hours and for a change, I felt content.

"Grace, I wanted to know if maybe you would like to go out for dinner sometime soon?"

I was not expecting this, but I was not interested in anything more with Maxwell. I did not want to hurt his feelings, but regardless of tonight, he still seemed slightly creepy in a nerdy kind of way.

"Listen, Maxwell, I enjoyed your company tonight, but I don't want to lead you on. I am not interested in any relationship right now. I hope you understand."

"Hey, wait a minute; dinner does not mean a relationship. I just wanted to have dinner and nothing more." Wow, I felt like an idiot.

"I apologize for making that assumption. I am not sure when I would be available for dinner, but I will let you know."

Maxwell got up to leave but hesitated for a moment. He turned and looked at me with intense eyes.

"Don't always skim the pages of the book. Make sure you take time to read the book. Good night and hope to talk to you sooner than later."

That left me speechless, and I was not quite sure what or why he made that statement. After Maxwell went home, I decided to turn in early because tomorrow was Jose Lopez day of reckoning.

I got to the warehouse around 8 am and Jose looked sickly; mostly because he was thirsty and hungry.

"Hey, it has been at least two days, and I have not had anything to drink or eat. I am feeling sick to my stomach. You have made your point. Please let me go."

I did not answer him. I pulled out the vial of succinylcholine and laid it on a small portable rolling tray, along with some latex gloves and a syringe.

"What is that you got there? Look I will admit that I am not a tough guy. I don't want to die. I am scared of dying. I am begging you to please let me go. I will do anything you say just please don't kill me." Tears were rolling down the side of his face.

"Wow the gangbanger, drug dealing thug is nothing more than a punk. You are not that tough after all. You are tough when attacking helpless women. Where is that toughness now? When committing your crimes did you ever think that you would pay for your crimes someday? No, don't answer that because it is evident that you never gave thought to reap what you sow. I find it so very difficult to muster up any sympathy for you. The only thing I can visualize is you sticking that knife repeatedly into my mother as she cried out for you to spare her life. Similar to your pleas right now. Your pleas are falling on deaf ears."

I put on the gloves and picked the vial and filled the syringe. I walked over to the table.

"I know that what I am about to do is selfish because it will not bring my mother back, but I will feel that you are paying for your sins."

I took the syringe and injected the poison into his arm. Within seconds his body seized up. It was as if an invisible pillow was over his face and I looked him directly in the eyes as I watched all the air being sucked out of him. Finally, his body went limp, and he was dead. I just stood there taking in the moment. I felt nothing, and I was not sure what I was supposed to feel.

I cleaned up all signs of my being there and removed the handcuffs and chains from Jose. I planned to leave his body there. I used an alias to rent the warehouse and paid with a money order. I paid a crackhead to go to the post office and purchase the money order. There was no way to trace the warehouse rental to me. I covered all of my tracks. As I left the warehouse, I looked at his body lying there and hoped that his soul would burn in hell.

7

WHO IS NICK?

*W*hen I got home, I took a long relaxing bubble bath. I was still not sure how I felt. Nick was next on my agenda. I was not sure how I was going to handle him, but he was unquestionably next. I checked in with my dad and decided I would be going back to work. I called my Captain Stark to let him know I was ready to return to work. He said I needed to meet with the company shrink to get clearance. This requirement was routine, and I had no problem with it. I was cleared with no problem and ready to get back to work. My only problem was I was not excited about working with Nick. I was not sure how I was going to handle him yet. I would take my time and feel him out and try to find out as much as I could, and I would then decide how I would handle him. I picked up the phone to dial Nick, but it started ringing.

"Hello."

"Hey, partner! I got word that you were jumping back into the saddle."

"You heard right, and I will be in the office tomorrow."

"Well, let's celebrate! Do you feel like going out for some drinks?" Even though I had no plans of leaving the house, I decided tonight was the best time to start figuring out Nick.

"Give me thirty minutes, and I will be ready."

"Alright, see you then." I need to be very careful with Nick because he was no fool and a good detective.

I got dressed, and when Nick arrived we decided to drive my truck, and Nick left his car at my house. We went to Pollos Mario Steak and Seafood restaurant on Franklin Street in Hempstead. We both order a glass of wine while we waited for our dinner.

"Surprised to see you are drinking wine. Thought you would have ordered a beer."

"I decided to show a little class tonight."

It was Wednesday night, so there was a light crowd. Our food did not take long to come.

"So, what have you been up to since I have I have been on leave?"

"Busy cleaning up the mess that the criminals leave behind."

"Have you heard anything regarding my mother's case?"

"Unfortunately, nothing yet but you know I will be the first one to let you know when I do."

I bet you would. We continued our meal, and I just made small talk. I was thinking about paying a visit to Joyce. Joyce was Nick's ex-girlfriend. They were supposed to get married, but she suddenly called it off. Joyce and I got along very well, but I never had a reason to pry into their relationship until now. Their breakup was very bitter, and I was sure I could talk to her in confidence. I would call her when I got home tonight. We finished our meal and talked a little longer, and I drove home.

"Well, I will see you tomorrow partner?"

"Goodnight Nick."

I went in the house before he could get a chance to kiss me on the forehead as he usually did. I immediately called Joyce, and she answered on the second ring.

"Hello."

"Hi, Joyce. This is Grace Noble. Do you remember me? I am Nick's partner."

"Yes, I remember you. Is something wrong with Nick?"

Her remark was not sympathetic in tone. It was more like, why are you calling me?

"No there is nothing wrong with Nick. I was wondering if we could meet up because I need to talk with you?"

"What is this about? Nick?"

I did not want to give her a reason to say no.

"Listen this has nothing directly do with Nick, and I need to speak in confidence. I figured since you and Nick are not talking I could trust you to keep our conversation in confidence."

There was an uncomfortable silence as if she was thinking it over.

"Ok, I can meet you tomorrow. Where did you want to meet?"

"Do have a problem if I stop by your house? I just did not want to chance running into Nick?"

"That's fine with me, and I should be home by six o'clock."

"Talk to you then." I was not sure what I was going to uncover by meeting with Joyce, but I was willing to try. I thought I knew everything about Nick but seems like I was wrong.

My first day back at work was slow and uneventful.

"Hey Nick, I will be leaving a little early today

because I have a six o'clock appointment with my father."

"No problem, just go and enjoy time with your dad."

I finished up around five o'clock and drove directly to Joyce's house. Joyce lived in Newark, New Jersey. The drive was going to be about an hour, and I would arrive around six o'clock. As I was driving I was trying to figure how to present my questions about Nick to her. I was hoping that because of how bad their breakup was she would be willing to spill all. Joyce lived in the Forest Hill section of Newark. Joyce owned a beautiful five-bedroom home on Grafton Avenue. She was a partner with a very successful law firm. She dated Nick for three years before they split up. Nick never told me the real reason for their breakup. His just said that they discovered that they were not compatible. As I pulled into her driveway, she came to the door before I got out of the car.

"Hi, Grace."

"Hi, Joyce. Thank you for agreeing to see me."

"Come in the house."

As we walked into the house, I could not help but notice how beautiful her home was. We went into the sitting room.

"Would you like something to drink? I have wine, water, beer, or pop."

"I will take water, thank you."

She got the water for me and wine for herself. She cut to the chase.

"So, what is it you wanted to talk about?"

"Well, I needed to talk about Nick. I don't think I know him as well as I thought."

She smirked and took a sip of her wine.

"Well, I guess you are finally seeing the real Nick."

I did not want to get into a conversation about their relationship. I was not sure what I wanted to find out, but I had to try.

"What do you mean by that? I have always felt like Nick was family, but lately, I am not so sure."

"Family? Really? You were never family to Nick. Nick hates you, and he is envious of you."

I was not sure I was hearing correctly or rather I could not believe what I was hearing. Did she hate Nick that much that she would lie on him?

"Don't look so shocked. Do you know how often I would have to hear him rant about you and your family? He would talk about how spoiled you were, and you had such a know it all attitude."

"Yes, I am shocked because my family treated Nick like family."

Deep down I knew she was telling the truth because

the Nick I thought I knew would not have been meeting with the man that killed my mother.

"I know you are shocked and I thought twice about telling you the truth. But evidently, you discovered something about Nick that has you second guessing him. All I can tell you is watch your back because he is not who he seems to be, and this is not a scorned woman talking. One other thing you should know is Nick has a serious cocaine habit. That was the major reason for our split."

"How could I have missed that?"

"He was the best functioning drug addict I know. Don't beat yourself up because he was good at deceiving people."

"How do you work with someone that long and you don't know them at all? Joyce can this conversation stay between you and I?"

"Who am I going to tell? But you have my confidence."

"Well, I am going to go now and thank you for taking that time to talk to me."

"No problem and please be careful."

8

MORE GOODBYES

I felt like I drove home in a trance. When I got home, I took a long hot shower. As the water ran down my back, I realized that Nick had to die. It was clear to me what I needed to do. The fact that he was meeting with the man that killed my mother meant he was somehow involved. I may never know the exact connection, but Nick has been lying to me, and he was guilty of something. He had to die. That other voice inside of me wanted to know what was I thinking. I vowed to protect and serve, but here I am talking about killing someone again. But I knew that Nick had to die, and he would die. My phone woke me up.

"Hello."

"Hey partner, we got a body."

When he gave me the address to a Queens warehouse, I already knew it was Jose.

"I will be right there."

"Hey Grace, you should know that the body belongs to Jose Lopez."

I did not respond and hung up. I looked at the clock to see that it was six in the morning. I got dress and headed to the scene. When I got there, Nick was by his car smoking a cigarette.

"What do we have?"

"It is weird; it looks like an apparent heart attack. But not sure what he was doing at this abandoned warehouse. We are going to try and get in touch with the owner but it is not adding up."

"Yeah, I see what you mean. Weird that a young gangbanger dies of a heart attack in an abandoned warehouse. Am I going loose any sleep over this one? Don't think so!"

"I understand, but I thought you would want to know about this one. Are you ok?"

"Yeah, I am ok, but I wish I could have been here when he drew his last breath. Well, let's get this one cleaned up."

It did not take us long because there was no evidence other than victim having a heart attack.

"Hey, before you leave, did you wonder why he was laying on the table?"

"Probably laid down when he could not breathe. And honestly Nick, I don't care. I am out of here."

As far as I was concerned, this was a closed case. Instead of going home, I went to the station to clean up some paperwork that had been sitting on my desk. I just could not get what Joyce told me out of my head. All this time I never knew the real Nick. I thought that he loved me, but instead, he hated me. Did his hate for me have anything to do with my mother's death? I needed to get some answer before killing him, but I needed to come up with a plan that would allow me to subdue Nick and talk to him before killing him. I would use the same drug I used on Jose, and they will conclude he had a heart attack. The fact that he is using cocaine will also make a heart attack believable. I felt like I was spiraling out of control. Despite feeling this way, I could not stop. I was dispensing my brand of justice, and they all had to pay.

I could not go back to the warehouse since they discovered Jose's body there. Then it dawned on me; I could go to Nick's house. Since it was going to look like a heart attack, that would be the perfect place. I just need to find a drug that I could slip to him that would immobilize him. I did some research and decided on

Nimbex which is a Neuromuscular blocking agent. It takes 90 seconds to take effect and last for 60 to 80 minutes. Enough time to have a one on one with Nick. I made a call to one of my informants, Randy, and put in an order for Nimbex. I had done so many favors for Randy, that there was no questions or hesitation when I needed a favor. Now I needed to find a day to carry out my plans. Nick was at the station, so I called him over to my desk.

"Hey, how about we do a movie night. We have not done one of those in a long time. I will bring the drinks; you can supply the food and the movies."

"You are funny, but I am game. How about Sunday since we both are off. Your house or mine?" "

Let's do your house because last time was mine and I don't feel like cleaning up behind you." "

That works for me. Any particular movies you want to see?"

"I will let you surprise me."

I went home around eight o'clock, and there was a note taped to my front door. I didn't have to open it to know it was from Maxwell. I grabbed the note and went into the house. I sat down and opened the envelope. There was a card in the envelope, and the only thing it said was "My passion is to tell stories that reflect humanity, by Pamela Grier." Who sent this to me? I thought it was from Maxwell, but there was no name on the card. This was weird and a little unsettling. I could not focus on this right now. I stuck the note in my desk drawer. It was time to relax and unwind. I started thinking about what I did and what I was about to do. I was not remorseful, scared or apprehensive. I felt at peace with my decision. Does that make me a psychotic murderer or a mental case? I was not sure and did not care. I felt like I was dispensing necessary justice. I know I was not God and there will be a day that I must answer for my sins, but I would deal with that when the time came. I suddenly thought about the girl that was murdered and her name was Pamela. The reason I thought about that was the note had a quote by Pamela Grier. Most knew Pamela Grier as Pam Grier, but there seemed to be an emphasis on Pamela. I must be losing my mind because I was just reaching for connections that were probably not there. I need to clear my mind and prepare for movie night with Nick.

The next few days were uneventful. I thought I would probably have an epiphany and come to my senses but that did not happen. I was determined to move forward with my plans for Nick. It was Sunday and I was ready for my meeting with Nick. I stop by the liquor store to pick up a bottle of wine and some beer. Surprisingly, I was not nervous. I was calm and ready. I rang his doorbell and there I stood face to face with the man I did not know.

"Hey sunshine, come on in."

"I brought you some beer and wine for myself. What are we eating?"

"I am making tacos."

"That's cool and I will make the drinks while you are cooking. I assume you will drink your beer from the bottle."

"That would be correct."

I went into the kitchen where Nick was cooking and got a glass for my wine. My back was facing Nick as I opened his beer and poured the Nimbex into his beer.

"Are the tacos finished?"

"Yes, they are and ready to go."

Well come and sit down for a minute and have a drink with me. We have some catching up to do because since I have been back we have not had a lot of time to chat it up."

He grabbed his beer and we went into the living room. He began drinking his beer. After two sips, he started to look a little agitated. I made a toast to encourage him to drink some more and he did.

"Hey Grace, I am starting to feel funny. It is like my whole body is going numb. This is weird and scary. Maybe you better call the paramedics."

"Really are you sure or maybe it is the beer and you are getting a buzz?"

"Hey, I am serious! I can't move, and it is as if I am paralyzed. What the hell is happening? I can't move at all."

The feeling I had at this moment was a feeling of power. He was under my control and it felt good. I got up from the couch and moved the coffee table out of the way as he watched. I got a chair out of the kitchen and sat it right in front of Nick.

"What are you doing? Grace, I am not kidding please get me some help because I am totally paralyzed."

"Help will be on the way shortly but first we have some things we need to discuss."

Suddenly, it was as if realization cover his face. He realized, without saying a word, that it was me who was responsible for his current situation.

"Grace, why?"

"Oh, don't you worry, the answer will come shortly. The drug I gave you will not kill you it will just keep you immobilized for a while. We are going to have a question and answer session and whether you live, or die will depend on your answers. Now do you have any questions before we begin?"

"Grace, have you lost your mind. What do you mean

by live or die? I have been like family to you and this is what you do to family?"

"No, I don't do this to family. In case you forgot, you despise me and my family. For so many years I thought you loved me like family only to find out you have been lying the whole time. I am not sure why you hate me Nick, but I have never given you a reason to hate me."

"Where the hell are you getting this from? I don't hate you and I never have. Oh my god, you have been talking to Joyce. That lying bitch. You can't trust anything she tells you. She was always jealous of our friendship, so she would say or do anything to destroy it."

"Well if I believe you and not her, then I have another interesting question for you; What was your relationship with Jose Lopez?"

"I have no idea what you are talking about. That is the guy who murdered your mother and I have no relationship to him at all."

"Nick, let's drop all the pretense because if I ask the question, you know I have evidence. I saw you talking to him. He got in your car and you did not arrest him. You guys had a conversation and he got out of your car and left. The man that murdered my mother! Explain this to me Nick."

I got up and started searching his apartment as he

could do nothing but watch. In his bedroom nightstand, I found about an ounce of cocaine. I walked back into the living room and dangled the baggy in his face.

"I guess you have a prescription for this?"

He was silent. I pulled out the syringe with the drug that would suck the life out of Nick.

"Talk to me Nick or die in silence. I need answers and I need them now."

"Look I have a little drug problem and I was into this dealer for some money. Jose was part of his gang I did not want to draw attention to myself by arresting him."

"Nick, I have been in the game too long for you to run bullshit on me. Come better than that."

"Well one thing you got right is I can't stand your uppity ass. For years I had to hear Captain tell me I could learn a thing or two from Grace. Always how perfect you were and hearing about your daddy the Judge. I did not have no one to pull strings for me. I had to work my ass off to get to where I am today."

"And just where is that Nick; a lying junkie police detective?"

"Don't judge me because not everyone is perfect like little miss Grace! You damn right I hate you and you will not find anything else out from me."

"You hated me enough to have my mother killed?" His eyes widened as if he had seen a ghost.

"You think I was responsible for that? It goes much deeper than you will ever know."

I was tired of hearing him and I realized what ever secret he was protecting, he was willing to take it to his grave. I did not get answers I was looking for, but I did get confirmation about Nick's feelings towards me. I picked up the syringe.

"So, little miss perfect will be nothing but a murderer after all."

"Nick I never claimed to be perfect but to rid the world of Jose and you brings more satisfaction than you will ever know."

His eyes widened once again, and he gasped in disbelief.

"That was you? You killed Jose?"

I took the syringe and held his arm and injected him with his death sentence.

"Say hello to Jose when you meet him in hell. Rest in turmoil!"

I watched as he took his last breath. I picked up the phone and called 911. "

This is detective Noble and I have an emergency. My partner is having a heart attack. I have tried to revive him, but he is unresponsive. Can you send help as soon as possible?"

I removed all incriminating evidence and returned

the cocaine to where I found it. I disposed of his beer and the bottle. I opened another beer and pour a little out and place on the table. There would probably be no investigation, but I did not want to take any chances. I needed to make sure that this would not be traced back to me. I was sad because I still was no closer to finding out what Nick's connection was with Jose. But it was time for me to move on. The paramedics arrive and pronounced him dead at the scene.

9

KEITH

*O*ver the next few weeks I felt like things were getting back to some form of normal. My father seemed to be adjusting to life without mom. I was not immediately assigned a new partner and I was ok with that. I kept busy working and I did not give any thought to Nick or Jose. It was business completed as far as I was concerned. I decided to have dinner by myself on a Friday after work. I made reservations at Delmonico's, located in the Wall Street area. I wanted to treat myself to a nice quiet dinner. It was slightly odd for me because I was the only one dining alone. But I did not care. I ordered my food and I was checking my email when someone said, "Excuse me." I looked up and staring back at me was a handsome man with bronze skin and piercing eyes. I could tell he had a muscular physique and the prettiest white teeth.

"I hate to bother you, but I had a reservation and they restaurant overbooked and looks like all tables were taken, and I noticed that you are dining alone. Would it be ok if I joined you? I promise not to talk you to death." There were two other men standing back behind him.

"Is it just you?" As I asked the question, I looked back at the other two gentlemen.

"Yes, it is just me. I am a United States Senator and those two are with me but won't be joining us for dinner."

I did want to eat alone but I decided to do my civic duty.

"Yes, you can join me, but I already ordered my food."

He smiled and jokingly responded, "I don't mind watching you eat."

"Do you have a name?"

"I apologize, my name is Keith Durham."

I guess he expected me to know who he was. I was not into politics and did not keep up.

"My name is Detective Grace Noble."

"Ok, letting me know you don't play up front. I appreciate that."

He was correct, I wanted him to know right off who

I was. Just as he was sitting down, they brought out my food.

"Since my food is here, why don't you tell me a little about yourself while I eat."

That was his opening because he told me more than a little. He told me his whole life story. It was as if he was waiting to tell his story to someone. I must admit, I enjoyed the company and he was pleasant to be around.

At the close of our dinner he asked, "Do you mind going out to dinner with me soon. Maybe next week?"

I was not expecting that invite but I said yes. I could not remember the last time I went on a date. I guess you could call this an official date. We exchanged phone numbers and he told me he would call later in the week. Then I mentally put my defenses up; he won't call me. Over the next couple of days, I could not get Keith out of my mind. I thought about him constantly. This was not like me, but I could not help it. I started to call him but decided against it because I did not want to come off as needy. I was feeling like a school girl waiting to go on my first. He called me the following Wednesday and we confirm our Saturday dinner arrangements. We talk for about twenty minutes. It was easy talking to him. Our dinner date was wonderful, and we enjoyed each other's company. I invited him over to my place for drinks, but he declined.

"I would love to have a nightcap with you, but I have an early flight to Washington. I will be in Washington for a week, but I would love to get together when I return and take you up on that nightcap."

I was falling hard and fast for this guy, but I still needed to play it cool. For the first time, I was allowing myself the happiness of being with a man. I did what any detective would do; I ran a background check on Senator Keith Durham. I needed to make sure there were no hidden secrets. His background check came back clean. My father also noticed the change in me.

"Hey princess, what is going on with you? There is a glow I have never seen before."

"Dad, it is nothing. I am just busy at work."

"I would not call a man nothing."

We started laughing because I could not fool my dad. He knew me so well.

"So, when do I get to meet this man?"

"Way too soon. I just went on one date and it will be a while."

"Well I will be waiting, and I am glad to see you happy for a change. How have you been doing since Nick's death?"

"I have been doing good. I miss him, but I am ok"

I did not tell my father about the real Nick, so I had to fake my missing him.

"I hope they get you a partner soon because I don't like you out here alone."

"I will be fine, and I should have a partner soon."

Keith and I had been dating for six months, and we were in an exclusive relationship. I never saw myself being in a serious relationship, but I was happy. Keith was back and forth to Washington, but that was ok with me because that gave me the space I needed. My doorbell rang, and I knew it was not Keith because he was in Washington. I looked out the peephole, and to my surprise it was Maxwell. I was surprised because I had not seen Maxwell since I was dating Keith. I just assumed he saw Keith coming and going.

"Hey Maxwell, how are you?"

"I am good and you?"

"I am good also. Do you want to come in?"

"Yes, thank you."

He came in, and I offered him a beer. We made small talk for a while.

"I wanted to tell about this woman who was around here looking for anyone who knew something about a woman named Pamela."

That was the name of the young lady we found dead after we found her at the scene of a murder. But who would be looking for info on her, especially around here?

"What else did she say?"

"She just said she was looking for anyone that can let her know how Pamela die."

But how did she know to look in this neighborhood? Something was not right.

"Can you describe this woman?"

"Yes, I can."

He gave me a description, but it was not familiar to me. This was unsettling because it was as if the past was creeping back into my present. I was not sure who this woman was and had nothing else to go on.

"Maxwell, if this woman returns, will you call me right away?"

"Yes, I will. I would have come over sooner, but I saw you had company and I did not want to disturb you."

"That is my boyfriend, and you can contact me even if he is here."

Maxwell did not look surprised when I said that Keith was my boyfriend. I guess he assumed that he was my boyfriend based on the frequency that he visited me.

"I will let you know if she comes around again."

When Maxwell left, I thought about Pamela again. What was the deal with this girl? I had no leads and nothing to investigate.

SO MANY TEARS

*O*ver the next couple of days, I did not hear from Maxwell. I was hoping to hear that the woman showed up again asking about Pamela. It was a slow Saturday, and I was bored. Keith was not due to get back home until Sunday. He called me in the morning, and we talked for forty-five minutes. I enjoyed our conversations, but I was glad he would be home Sunday. My phone rang.

"Hello"

"Hey Grace, I need you down at the station. I sent Roman over to pick you up."

That was odd because I had my vehicle.

"That is not necessary. I would rather drive my car. And why would you send someone for me? What's going on Captain?"

"Please trust me on this one and ride with Roman. I will explain everything once you get here."

Just as he hung up, my doorbell rang.

"Hey Roman, I am ready. What is going on and why did Captain send you to pick me up?"

"I don't know Grace. Captain just called me and said pick you up."

When we got to the station, I went straight to Captain's office.

"Hey Captain, what's up?"

"Please close the door." I closed the door and sat down.

"I did not want you to hear this on the radio or the news. I am so sorry to have to bring you this news."

Oh, would you please get to the point. My stomach was now in knots.

"Your father was shot and killed this afternoon."

Ok, I must not have heard the captain correctly. There must have been a mistake.

"What did you say?"

"Grace, I am so sorry. We are doing everything possible to catch the person responsible."

I felt like I just got shot. I could not breathe and my head started spinning. I passed out. I woke up in the hospital emergency room.

"Miss Noble, I am Dr Grassi." I got up and started putting on my jacket.

"Miss Noble, you should take it easy." I started to walk out the room and turn to face the doctor.

"I am fine, and I am leaving."

I left the hospital and caught a taxi back to the station. I knocked on the captain's office door.

"Captain, I need to talk to you."

"Grace, what are you doing here? You should be at the hospital."

"I am fine. I just need to know what happened." He sat down as if he was defeated.

"Your father was leaving the courthouse and as he was about to get into his truck, a car drove by and started shooting. He was pronounced dead at the scene."

"Where was he shot and how many times?"

"Grace, you…"

I cut him off before he could finish.

"I need to know all of it."

"He was shot 12 times, and one of the bullets pierced his lung."

I could not feel anything right now. I was numb and trying to process what I just heard. My phone started ringing, and I step out of the captain's office to take the call.

"Grace, I just saw the news. Are you alright?"

"Am I alright? You are asking me, am I alright? Keith, I may never be alright again. My whole family has been taken from me. First my mother and now my father."

"Let me come and get you. You don't need to be alone right now."

I wanted to be alone, but Keith was an exception. I wanted or needed him to hold me and tell me that everything was going to be alright.

"I am at the police station."

"Stay there and I will be right there to get you."

He picked me up and we went to his apartment. He did not say much. He put on some very soft music and just held me. I cried for the first time since hearing the news. I cried for my mother and my father. I felt so lost, but I was already thinking about how I would kill the person responsible. They had to pay with their life. I had turned in the same murderers that I hunt. I knew no matter how I justified it, I was still as guilty as the criminals I sought. But I did not care because only thing I could see was vengeance. I stayed with Keith that night, but I was up early the next morning on the phone making arrangements for my father. When Keith got up, he came into the living room where I was.

"What are you doing up so early?"

"I needed to start making the arrangements for my father's funeral."

"Please let me help you. Just tell me what is needed."

I did allow Keith to help me with the funeral and I was grateful for his help because as I was moving through the process, I found out that I was not so strong after all. The day of the funeral was one of the hardest days of my life. My parents were my world and now both were gone. I did not know how my life could be complete without them. Keith was my rock. He was at my side the whole time and did not leave me. He cancelled his Washington trip just to be my support.

There were some leads in the case, but Captain refused to give me any information because I was personally involved. That was ok because I had some detective buddies that were willing to keep me in the loop. They were looking for Jose Lopez's brother for questioning. They believe this was related to Jose's case because Jose's family thought that he was murdered even though the medical evidence states he had a heart attack. They believe it had something to do with my mother's death and that is why they targeted my dad. They were partially correct. Now on top of my grief, I felt responsible for my father's death. If I had not kill Jose, my father would still be alive. Jose's brother's name was Victor Lopez, and Victor Lopez was going to die. The only problem was he was being held in county lockup, and I would have to wait it out. But no matter how long I would have to wait, Victor Lopez was going to die.

MORE QUESTIONS

Keith and I were getting more serious. I was in love with Keith. I did not tell Keith I was in love with him, but I think he knew how I felt. Keith was a distraction from all the hurt and pain. When I was with Keith, I could escape my reality. Reality is I am a murderer, and no matter how I tried to justify it, I am a murderer. I hated to think of myself as a murderer, but that was my reality. And here I was prepared to murder again. I decided to do something that I could not let Keith or my captain know I was doing. I was going to visit Victor Lopez because I needed answers. I needed to know why he killed my father before I took his life. Keith was scheduled to go to Washington in two days so that would be the perfect time to pay a visit to Victor.

As I entered Rikers Island and I heard gates closing behind me, I got this eerie feeling of doom and dread. I never liked visiting prisons because of the way they made me feel. I saw dead bodies all the time, but I never felt like I did when visiting a prison. Part of this feeling was when those gates closed; I felt like I have lost control. I was under someone else's control. I needed to be in control always. I had a seat in the visitor's room while they went to get Victor. I was very anxious because I was ready to get answers from Victor. Why my father? It was never stated that his brother was murdered, so why kill my father. The autopsy on his brother indicated he died from a heart attack, so why blame my family or me. I needed to understand why he killed my father. My whole world snatched from me, and I needed answers. As they were bringing Victor in, all I saw was a little boy. He looked no older than sixteen, but he walked with a smugness that said he feared nothing. I was finally facing my father's murderer.

"Victor, do you know who I am?"

He was fidgeting in his seat and had a look of disdain on his face.

"No, am I supposed to know you?"

I could tell this was not going to be easy.

"My name is Detective Grace Noble." I paused for a few seconds to let the introduction sink in.

"So, what do you want with me?"

"My father was Judge Noble, the man that you killed. I just need to know one thing from you, why?"

"Why what? Why did I kill him?"

He was very arrogant, and there was not an ounce of remorse on his face.

"I killed him because I was following orders."

"What do you mean you were following orders? Someone told you to kill my father?"

He sat up in his chair and looked me square in the eyes.

"You have no idea what is going on. There is more to this than you know, and I am sure in due time, you will put the pieces of the puzzle together. Don't bother asking me who because you will not get any more out of me."

My head was spinning because I could not understand what was going on.

"I thought you killed my father because of your brother's death." He looked slightly surprised.

"Now why would I do that? My brother died of a heart attack. Look, lady, I don't have anything else to say to you."

He called for the guard, and he went back to his cell.

My head was in a fog and could not remember how I got home. Who wanted my father dead? Was Victor telling me the truth? He had no reason to lie to me. He seemed genuinely surprised when I mentioned him killing my father because of his brother's death. I had more questions than previously.

MAXWELL

I got home, and there was a letter taped to my door. I knew before looking that it had to be Maxwell. He was the only one that would have left a note on my door. I went inside and sat down to read his note. It was short and straight to the point. It said,

"I need to see you as soon as possible."

Alright, I guess it was necessary for me to re-establish boundaries with this guy. Matter of fact, I think it is time to tell Maxwell that he needs not ever contact me again. Just as I was about to call him, my cell phone rang.

"Hello"

"Did you get my note?"

It was Maxwell, but his whole tone was different. It

was not that meek and timid Maxwell I knew. It was a more aggressive Maxwell.

"Yes, I got your note, and I was about to call you."

"Well, when can we meet?"

Not sure what had gotten into Maxwell, but I did not want to be bothered.

"Look, Maxwell, I will not be meeting you, and I would appreciate it if you did not contact me anymore."

"I will contact you when I need, and you will meet with me."

Ok, this man has lost his mind. I knew I should have put him in his place a long time ago.

"Maxwell not sure what is going on with you but I am not meeting with you, and if you continue to contact me, I will get a restraining order."

He chuckled as if he found me amusing.

"You will not be getting a restraining order, and you will be meeting with me real soon. Since your boyfriend is out of town, I think I will stop over now."

"Listen you have lost your mind. If you step foot on my property, I will have you arrested. Do you understand me?"

"I wonder did Jose Lopez understand or did your partner understand?" There was a moment of uncomfortable silence.

"I don't know what you are talking about, but I am done with this conversation."

I hung up the phone. I just sat on my couch stunned. What did he mean? What did he know? I was 100% sure that I covered all my tracks. And what with this new found aggressive attitude. Who did he think he was threatening me? I hated to feel like I was not totally in control. Maybe I was getting nervous and upset for no reason. Maybe he just referenced Jose and my partner because he was jealous. He knew how close I was with Nick. That had to be it because there is no way he could know. Now I needed to see him and find out exactly what he knew and what did he want. I dialed his number, and the phone rang once.

"So, should I come over now?"

He was arrogant and cocky. This was not the Maxwell that I knew.

"Yes, come over now."

I kept my revolver on me just in case he tried something. I was nervous because I did not know what I was dealing with at this moment. Five minutes later, my doorbell rang. I opened the door and was taken aback because it was Maxwell but then again it was not. He did not have on his usually preppy nerdy clothes. He stood dressed very stylish, and he looked very handsome. He walked in and walked right past me and sat down in the living room.

"Ok, listen, Maxwell, I don't know what you think you know, and I don't appreciate you just barging in here like you own the place." He looks at me and starts smiling.

"Have a seat Grace. You are not in control this time. I am in control, and you will listen carefully to what I have to say. Yes, I know that you murdered Jose and Nick. The look of surprise on your face is priceless."

I decided I needed to sit down. How could he know and most importantly, what did he want?

"I know that you are asking how did I know? Well, let me answer that for you. I know because I was the puppet master. I was orchestrating everything, and it was me that was pushing all the right buttons to set this all-in motion. Now I will walk you through the how. I have studied you for many years, and I know you better than you know yourself. I knew if your mother was murdered you would seek revenge. I knew I could push you to murder. The only problem was the idiot that I got to do the job, did not kill her initially. But luck would have it; she died eventually. I then needed you to murder again and what perfect way to accomplish that by exposing your friend Nick for the scum that he was. I knew if you saw Nick chatting it up with your mother's murderer, that would set you off. I knew your discovery of the real Nick was enough to get you to murder again. This was perfect because now you have two murders under your belt. You belong to me now."

I could not speak. I was totally lost for words and I just continued to listen.

"Now let's talk about the why. My father was a monster. He abused my mother both physically and mentally. She was worthless as a mother. She did not know how to protect us. My father beat me and my brother for breakfast, lunch and dinner. I was 14 and my brother was 7 years old. I ran away and promise I would come back for my brother. I did not get back in time before the beating turned into sexual assault. He sexually abused my brother for years. My brother was 14 years old when he finally had enough. He went into my father's closet and got his loaded handgun. He hid the gun until my father went to sleep. He went into my father's bedroom and shot my father in the head as he slept. I failed to protect my brother. My father had a daughter with another woman, and she testified at my brother's trial that her father was not abusive and my brother was lying and planned to kill his father because he was jealous. Can you believe the jury bought into her story? The forensic investigator testified that there was nothing to lead her to believe the murder was defensive.

In her opinion, it was premeditated. He was tried as an adult and found guilty of 2nd-degree murder and sentenced to 25 years to life in prison. A month later, my brother hung himself in his prison cell."

This was all beginning to sound familiar to me. I let him continue to talk.

"A month later, my mother took a gun and blew her brains out. Right before my eyes, my whole family is gone. Now I will connect the dots for you. The step sister's name was Pamela. Last name is not important. I think Pamela rings a bell for you. Pamela felt horrible for what she did, and she constantly contacted me asking for forgiveness. I finally told her that the only way I could forgive her was to do something for me. She was thrown in just to spook you a little. Now you know why she ended up with a bullet between the eyes. By now I guess you have figured out who the forensic investigator was. I found out from my brother's attorney that your testimony was the nail in my brother's coffin."

It was all crystal clear now.

"Maxwell, I am so sorry for all that you have lost but you can't blame me for this because I was only doing my job."

"Do you remember my mother trying to talk to you and make you understand that he was abused and raped. You chose to turn a blind eye to this information."

"So, you made me pay by taking my family from me? Was that your sick twisted way to get revenge? You won't get away with this!"

"Oh yes I will. I have already gotten away with it. You see you will never chance going to jail because if you turn me in then I will be forced to reveal who murdered Jose and Nick. Yes, this is my revenge. But it gets better. Your journey is not over. I see that you and the Senator are quite the item. Looks like your relationship has blossomed. When I lost my brother and mother, I had nothing and no one and I demand the same for you. Losing your mother and father by the hands of someone else was hard but image losing someone you love by your own hands. Think about that for a minute."

I was not sure what he was getting at, but I was tired and just wanted him to get to the point.

"What is your point Maxwell?"

"You are going to kill the dear Senator, your new love interest."

"I know you have lost your mind if you think I am going to kill Keith. I know you have lost a lot but this is not going to bring back your brother or mother. Is this something your mother would have wanted you to do?"

"Stop with the psychology bullshit! You will do this, and you have fourteen days to make sure the Senator is dead. And in case you plan on killing me instead; my lawyer has a file that he is instructed to open upon my death. That file contains some very interesting things including some comprising photos. You went to great extremes to cover your tracks but because you were not aware of the trap I was setting for you, there was plenty of opportunity for me to collect evidence. This is not up for negotiation or discussion. I don't care how you kill him. I just want him dead in two weeks. In two weeks if the Senator is still alive, you will spend the rest of your life in jail. So, you have a very important decision to make; my life or the Senator's life."

He stood up and stared at me for a few minutes.

"I will destroy you if It is the last thing that I do. One last thing, do even think about telling the Senator, because if you do I will kill him and I will meet you in jail."

He walked to the front door without looking back and left. I don't know how long I sat on that couch, but it felt like an eternity. How was I going to get out of this mess? He was right about one thing, there was no way I could go to jail. I could not think straight but I needed to figure this out before Keith got back into town in two days. I called my captain and requested the next two days off from work.

"Are you ok Grace? It is very rare that you take time

off. I know things have been very difficult lately but just want to make sure that you are ok."

"Captain, I am fine. I just have some things to take care regarding my father."

He was genuinely concerned about me and I understood. I needed to do some digging and find out what I could about Maxwell. I guess I would start with digging up information on his brother's trial.

13

MORE CONFUSION

I found information about the trial. Maxwell's brother's name was Kevin. The thing that was puzzling was there was no physical evidence of abuse. Expert doctors were not able to find any evidence of abuse. This was one factor that went against him at the trial. I could not find out much about the mother except she had a sister name, Evelyn. I found contact information for Evelyn. She lived in Crown Heights section of Brooklyn. I decided I would pay a visit to her and see if I could get a better picture of who Anita Harrington was and what went wrong in that family. I decided I would not call Evelyn. I would just show up hoping she would talk to me.

I left to see Evelyn around 6 pm Friday evening. When I got to the apartment building where Evelyn lived, I thought that maybe I should have called first. I rang the buzzer for apartment 4C, and after no answer, I rang it again.

"Hello, who is it?"

"I am looking for Evelyn. This is Detective Grace Noble. I just wanted to...."

Before I could finish explaining what I wanted, she buzzed me in. I took the elevator to the fourth floor and her apartment was to the left of the elevator. She was standing in the doorway, waiting for me.

"Hi, I am Grace Noble."

"Come in and close the door behind you."

We walked down a short hallway past the living room and to the kitchen.

"Have a seat and tell me how I can help you. I assume it has something to do with my nephew."

"It is about your sister. I have been reviewing your nephew, Kevin's case and I am trying to understand the family dynamic to see...."

Once again, she cut me off before I could finish.

"Look lady, I don't know what your deal is and I don't care. I will be happy to tell you about my sister and her devil spawn children. But you must never tell Maxwell that I spoke to you. That one scares the hell out me. It was just the two of us, my sister and me. We grew up in Camden, South Carolina. I was the vocal sister and

Anita was the quiet introverted sister. Anita did not date in school and when she graduated, she met Ricardo and fell in love, or at least she thought she was in love. I never cared for Ricardo, because I sensed a slickness about him but he treated her good. They only dated a month before he dragged her down to City Hall and they got married."

She was was fidgeting with a piece of paper as she spoke. I was not sure if that was just a nervous habit.

"She was eighteen years old. My parents did not approve of her getting married so young but she was in love. She got pregnant a month after she got married. She was not ready to take care of a child and Ricardo was not working. My parents convinced them to give the child up for adoption so the child would stand a chance at a better life. It was hard for Anita to do but she gave her child up. A year later she got pregnant with Maxwell. He was always a very active child. When he was six years old I started to notice how manipulative he was. Very sneaky child. Seven years later she gave birth to Kevin. Kevin loved his older brother and in his eyes Maxwell could do no wrong. I was not the biggest fan of Ricardo in the beginning but he took care of his family."

I did not expect her to be so forthcoming with information but she had no problem talking.

"He did cheat on my sister and had a child with another woman. My sister forgave him. I never saw any signs that he was abusive to those boys. I can tell you this, they were so disrespectful to their father. He had a hard time raising them and when they found out about his affair, it got worst. But I believe those boys planned to kill their father and thought they would get away with it. When it did not work out that way, Kevin could not take being in prison and snapped. I know you are the woman who testify about the forensic evidence and I know your testimony was instrumental in convicting Kevin. Please don't feel bad because you were doing what was right. Those boys are not right. I am not sure why you really want this information but if it has anything to do with Maxwell, please be careful. He is very dangerous and after his brother killed himself, I think he got worst. He was very close to his brother. I am not sure why you are digging into this, but just watch yourself."

"I was wondering has anyone had any contact with the child that was given up for adoption?"

"No, I have never heard anything else." I stood up to leave.

"Thank you very much for seeing me."

She walked me to the door and I left. I was not sure how any of the information she provided would help me but it was good to have a background. Tomorrow was Saturday and Keith was due home and I was no further in figuring out how to handle Maxwell. I could not kill Keith but if my back was against the wall…. From my visit with Evelyn, I was beginning to feel that there was no abuse. And if there was no abuse, then why did Kevin kill his father? I did not have a lot of time to figure this out and I needed to know everything about Maxwell.

When I got home, there was a note taped to my door. I went inside and opened the letter.

I hope you are working on your plan. Maxwell

He was getting on my nerves, and I wanted to kill him!! I think my next step would be to pay a visit to his lawyer and see what I can find out. I would need to first break into his office after hours to see if I could locate this file that he mentioned. I found out that his lawyer was Edward Schawl. From what I have heard, he is a low life lawyer that represents the scum of the earth. I knew where his office was, but I needed to pay a visit late tonight and see if I could locate this file.

His office was on Seaview Avenue, in Canarsie, Brooklyn. I just wanted this nightmare to end. My phone was ringing. It was Keith.

"Hey babe, how are you?"

"I am good. I miss you, and I am glad I will be home tomorrow. I was calling to see if you would pick me up from the airport and maybe we could go to dinner afterwards."

"That sounds fine. What time does your flight get in?"

"I will arrive at 4:10 pm. Well, I must run. Love you!"

"Love you too." That was the first time I said I love you.

"That was nice to hear. I will see you tomorrow."

I realized that I did love Keith and I had no intention of killing him. Around 9 pm, I drove over to Edward Schawl office and parked outside. I could see the lights were on in his office, so I decided to keep watching until the lights went out and I saw him exit the building. At 9:35 pm the lights went out in the office. Two minutes later I saw Edward Schawl leaving the building. I waited for fifteen minutes before getting out of my car. I wanted to be sure that he would not return for something he forgot.

I entered the building and found his office. The lock was very easy to pick. Within minutes I was in his office. I used my flashlight instead of turning on the lights in the room. I did not need to draw attention. I searched his files for about 20 minutes, and I finally found a file with Maxwell's name on it. I opened the folder and examined the information that was in the folder. Maxwell was not lying. He documented everything and had pictures of me sitting in my car surveying Jose's goings and comings. There were pictures of me meeting with my drug supplier. He had enough information to raise a lot of suspicions and eventually land me in jail. Maxwell did his homework. I put the folder in my coat and closed his office up the way I found it. I left his office and drove to 930 Lincoln Place in Crown Heights, Brooklyn. I parked my car and put on my gloves. I pulled out a .45 calibre handgun and attached a silencer. I bought the handgun from a street dealer, and the exchange was not faced to face. I left the money an agreed upon location, and he did the same with the gun. There was no way to trace it back to me. I put it in my bag and got out of the car. I went up to the front door and rang the doorbell. Edward Schawl opened the door and asked, "How can I help you?"

I showed him the gun and backed him into his apartment. I gestured for him to sit on the couch. I then raised my arm and pulled the trigger. I shot him once in the head. I checked for a pulse to make sure he was dead. Even though I had on gloves, I still wiped the gun clean and laid it beside the dead body. I went out the back door and went all the around the block back to my car and left. I made sure no one saw me leaving his apartment. I could not think about who I had become. I was just concerned with protecting myself and ridding myself of Maxwell. Now with his lawyer dead and the evidence in my hand, Maxwell did not have a hold over me. But I still needed to get rid of Maxwell, and I needed to do it quickly.

14

KILLING BECOMES EASY

*E*ven though I just killed a man, I had a restful sleep when I got home. I decided I needed to get to Maxwell before Keith got home. I called Maxwell and informed him that I needed to see him.

"I was hoping that you were calling me to inform me that the Senator was dead."

"Not yet but I am working on it. He does not get back into town until tonight."

"I will be over there in a few minutes."

I took out my police issued revolver and put it in the waistband of my pants. I sat on the couch and waited for Maxwell to arrive. When my doorbell rang it startled me. I opened the door and gestured for him to come in. We went into the living room and he sat down. I sat down across from him.

"So, what is the purpose of this visit?" I looked him square in the eye with defiance. "I have not intentions on killing Keith."

"So, you don't believe that I have evidence that would incriminate you. I guess you need me to call my lawyer to verify that I have enough evidence to send you away for life."

As I sat and looked at Maxwell, I became more enraged.

"No need to call your lawyer, because Edward will not be taking any of your calls today or any other day."

A look of concern fell over his face. At that point, I pulled out my weapon and pointed it at him.

"Wait a minute! You don't want to do that because you would definitely seal your fate."

"I am not sure about that because by my calculations, this would solve all of my problems. No evidence and no Maxwell." His concern turned to panic.

"You really need to think this through carefully. How are you going to explain killing a man in your living room?"

"Oh, that is easy. Your constant visits, notes and phone calls show a pattern of obsession. I thought I could be nice to you but you became more delusional. You came over here today under the pretense of trying to apologize for being so pushy but instead you pulled a gun on me. You threatened me and you said that if you could not have me, then no one would. We would die together and be together in our afterlives. Hey that even sound convincing to me. I am good at this, don't you think?"

"I guess I underestimated you. Listen we can work something out."

I looked him straight in the eyes and pulled the trigger. Bullet pierced his heart and he was instantly dead. I check his pulse and then got busy setting up the crime scene. I placed a loaded gun in his hand to get his fingerprints on it. After I finished making sure everything was in place, I called the station in a frantic voice reporting the incident. Everything went as planned. I called Keith to let him know what happen and because of the investigation, I would not be able to meet him at the airport.

"That is fine. I am just glad that you are ok. I will get a taxi from the airport. I am coming straight to see you once I get home. I love you and I am so sorry you had to go through this and if you need anything please let me know."

"Thank you, Keith, and I love you too." I felt so relieved and I was glad that this nightmare has finally come to an end. All I wanted was to see Keith.

After the CSI team finished up, I headed over to the station to see Captain Wilks.

"Hey Captain, you wanted to see me?"

"Hey Grace, are you ok? You have gone through a lot lately, and I think you need to take a six-month leave and get yourself together. Also during that time, I want you to see a therapist."

"Really? Come on Captain. You know I can't stay out for six months, and I don't need to see a shrink. Don't make me do this" He was adamant and would not back down.

"Sorry, this has to happen, and it is protocol. Both your parents were murdered, your partner is dead, and a crazy neighbor tries to kill you. That's a lot. Take this time to relax and pamper yourself. You are one of my best detectives, and I need you on top of your game. That's an order."

I guess I was on an extended vacation. Maybe I could go with Keith the next time he goes to Washington. I called Keith and told him I would rather meet at his place because that dead man in my living room was still fresh in my head. I had to play the role.

"Listen, sweetheart, pack an overnight bag and come stay with me for a few days."

"I will do that, and I will see you in about 20 minutes."

I went home to pack a bag. I was excited to see Keith. Before I left, I sat down in the living room to take stock of all that had transpired starting with my mother's death. It was a crazy chain of events and to think that one person set all of this in motion. I thought about the fact that there was no evidence of abuse and if that was the case, what was the real motive behind the murder of Maxwell's father. That part still did not add up to me. But I was not going to wreck my brain because it was over. I also thought about my mother and father. I missed them so much. So much has changed in such a little amount of time. What would my father think of his daughter, the murderer? I want to believe he would have understood. There was a part of me that knew I walk with a badge of dishonor no matter how much I tried to justify those murders.

15

THE TRUTH PRESENTS ITSELF

I got to Keith's place around 7 pm. He had dinner waiting for me.

"I did not know that you could cook. Everything looks wonderful."

"After you eat I just want you to relax."

He made sirloin steak, green beans and baked potatoes. I had a glass of red wine with my dinner. After dinner, we went into the den.

"So, let me tell you a little bit about myself. It is unfortunate that I had to learn about you as you went through these difficult moments. I think it is important that we know each other and there are no surprises along the way."

"I thought you told me all about yourself that first night we met at the restaurant."

"Well, let me fill in some blanks for you. I am an only child and both my parents were in politics. That is public information and you probably already knew that. What is not public information is the fact that I am an adopted child. My birth mother gave me up right after I was born. I was told that I was adopted when I was 13 years old. I was angry at first because I could not understand why my mother would give me up. Don't get me wrong, my adopted parents were wonderful. As you can see, I did not want for anything. But that did not stop me from wanting to know. So, when I was in college, I decided I was going to search for my birth mother. When I finally found out who she was, I was surprised to find out that she had two children. I can't lie but I was angry. You gave me up, but you decide to keep and raise two other children that you had. Here is the kicker, all three of us had the same mother and the same father. When my birth mother and father got on their feet, why didn't they come looking for me? Do you have a child and just forget that they exist? I hired private detectives to learn all that I could about my family that discarded me."

I had never known Keith to sound so bitter.

"Well, my father took very good care of his family but that did not stop him from straying. He cheated on my birth mother and had a daughter with his mistress.

She eventually forgave him. You found forgiveness in your heart for your husband, but you never once wondered about that child you discarded. My two brothers seem to be doing fine. Only difference between them and me was they were getting the love that I never got a chance to experience. I guess you could say I developed a deep hatred for my brothers. I appreciated my adopted parents, but to know all of this made my days difficult. Then it got to the point that I felt like they should pay for making me feel so unwanted."

This was getting a little weird. And the fact that he was adopted, and Maxwell spoke of a brother that was given up at birth. Could this be?

"I see the look on your face but let me continue my story. I secretly began to despise the whole family. What I did find out was my brother, the oldest one, had gotten into some serious trouble with the mob and owed them a lot of money. I am sure you know what happens when you don't pay the mob. Well, he was ripe for the picking. I set my plan in motion. I would be the master manipulator and change the course of so many lives. I became drunk with power. I was able to wipe out two families without any connection to the crimes."

I was in a complete state of shock. It was Keith all the time. He was the true puppet master behind all of this.

"Don't say a word. Just let me finish. I am enjoying

the look on your face. You were a means to an end.
Brother Maxwell's greed allowed me to use him to set
things in motion. I know you were looking for a motive
for the killing of our father. The motive was hate. I
hated him and my birth mother. Oh, we can't forget
about the sweet stepsister Pamela."

I did not know what to say. I was devastated, heartbroken and angry all at once.

"You took my family from me. Why was I a part of
your sick plan?"

"That is easy to answer. Your father was the judge
who secretly arranged the adoption. And when my
mother hesitated about going through with the adoption, he was the one that convinced her that she was
doing what was best. Of course, he was good friends
with my adoptive parents at the time. So now you see
everyone's part in this play. And the best thing is that no
one can tie me to any of this. The adoption was sealed,
thanks to your dad. You became my ninja killing
machine and just made my escape easier."

"Do you honestly think I will let you get away with
this? I would rather spend the rest of my life in jail
before I see you go free."

I could not understand how I got so caught up in
this. At this point, I would except whatever my fate was.
He stood up and walked over to me and before I could

see the knife in his hand, it was already driven deep into my chest. There was a searing pain and I could see the blood running down the front of my blouse. Keith scooped me up and laid me on the couch and held me in his arms.

"Grace, I was never in love with you, but I did admire how you would stop at nothing to protect the people you loved. You were so distraught over the deaths of your parents and the death of your partner, who most believed he was like a brother to you. You finally snapped and could not go on any longer."

"No one would ever believe that I would commit suicide."

"Yes, but you typed up such a compelling suicide note. They will wonder how they missed the signs."

I felt life slipping from me. I was ok with dying because this was my penance. I felt at peace as the end drew near.

"Close your eyes precious Grace and sleep." I closed my eyes and I could see my father beckoning for me to come to him. Into his arms I ran.

Shannon Spruill was born and raised in Brooklyn, New York but now resides in Buffalo, NY. She is a wife to Deacon Esau Spruill, Jr. and mother to three sons. Shannon graduated Suma Cum Laude from Bryant and Stratton College with a bachelor's degree in Business Administration and a master's degree in Computer Information Systems from Boston University. She is currently working on her doctoral degree in Biblical

Studies. She is an Account Representative at Ingram Micro, where she has been employed for 22 years. Looking for a new road to travel, Shannon decided to pursue her lifelong desire to write her first book. She has always wanted to write fiction, but she felt she had a story to tell.

Shannon's first book was released December 1, 2010. "My Reflection in the Mirror" is a look at some personal demons that she had to overcome. She hoped by telling her story she would inspire and empower other women. October 4, 2013, Shannon lost her son, Brian in an automobile accident. This was a devastating tragedy but instead of sinking into a dark place, Shannon grieved and relied on her faith and trust in God. She began helping other parents that have lost a child. She started the Buffalo Chapter of Bereaved Parents of the USA. She also published her second book, "The Shattered Mirror: Picking up the Pieces." This book was about how she copes with the death of her son. Because she felt that both these books were her personal testimony, she combined both books and published them as one. In 2018, she gave the book a face-lift with a new book cover and title: "Tribulation to Victory: Birth of a Queen."

Shannon has several other books under her belt. She is also the CEO and Founder of SMS Write On Publishing, LLC and SMS Film & Media, LLC. Shannon is a former board member for the William-Emslie YMCA and Our Curls, Inc. She is also the convener of the Faith Missionary Baptist Church Women's Christian Fellowship Ministry. In March 2018, she received the award, "Women Touching the World", for her community work. With all of these responsibilities, writing remains one of her top priorities, second to serving God.